☆☆☆ ARLO & PIPS ☆☆☆

JOIN THE CROW CROWD!

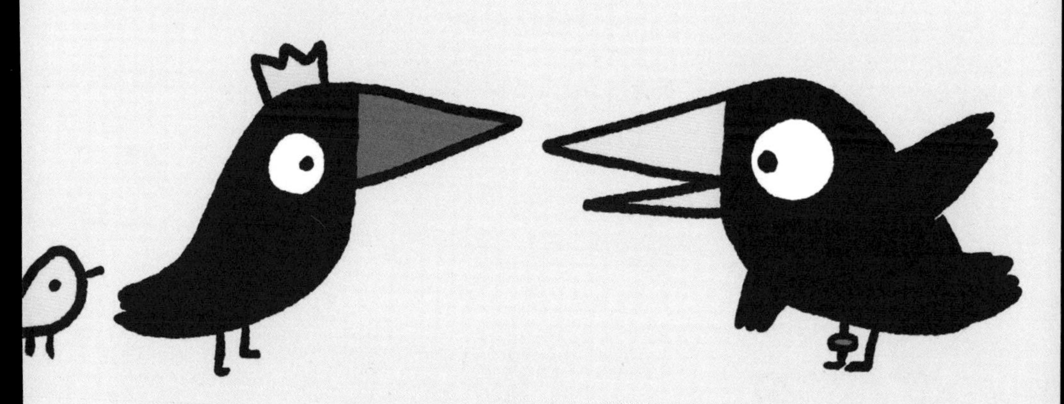

ELISE GRAVEL

An Imprint of HarperCollinsPublishers

HarperAlley is an imprint of HarperCollins Publishers.

Arlo & Pips #2: Join the Crow Crowd!

www.harperalley.com

Library of Congress Control Number: 2020950523
ISBN 978-0-06-239423-1 (trade bdg.) — ISBN 978-0-06-305077-8 (pbk.)

The artist used Photoshop to create the digital illustrations for this book.
Typography by Elise Gravel and Chrisila Maida
21 22 23 24 25 GPS 10 9 8 7 6 5 4 3 2 1

❖
First Edition

To Andrew Arnold

Hey, Arlo,
what's up?

Shhhh!

POK
HEY!

HA HA HA HA HA HA HA HA!

Ha ha ha! Did you see that guy's face?
It was so funny!

Are you throwing acorns at humans?

YES! Clever, huh?

No! And it's not very nice, either.

I know . . . but I'm so
BORED.

Well, let's find you something better to do.

Hmm . . . How about treasure hunting?

Nah . . . I have enough treasures.

ENOUGH TREASURES?

That's not like you, Arlo. Are you okay?

I don't know.

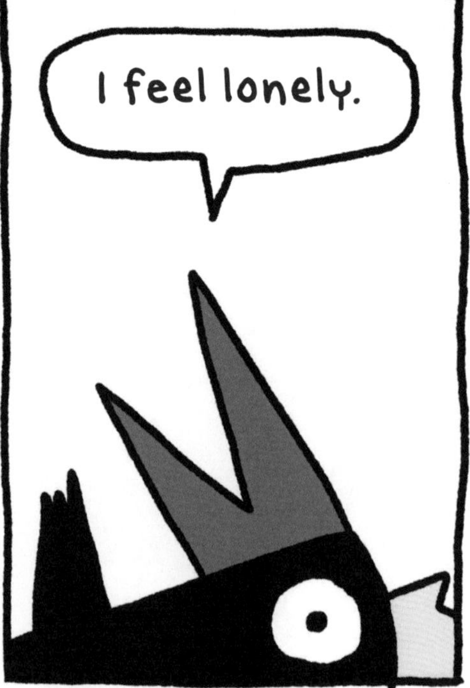
I feel lonely.

Crows are social birds, and they often live in groups.

And since I'm new in town,
I don't know any crows.

Can't you go visit your old
friends from the woods?

NEVER.

O-o-o-kay.
Why not?
One of them called me "poopyhead."
HA HA HA!
Oops, sorry.

Crows can hold a grudge for a very long time.

That's too bad.
Well, I guess you have to make new friends now.
Maybe I can help. There's a group of crows who live in the park.

That's true! Weird, huh?

In certain cultures, crows are known as "tricksters." Others believe they bring bad luck or are a bad omen.

Well, you DO throw acorns at them.

I was bored, okay? Besides, acorns are not dangerous.

Anyway, where do these guys live?

I'll show you. Follow me.

THE
PARK

That's true. Like this book, for instance.

There they are.
OOH!

Go talk to them!

I'm shy. There are too many of them.

Start with one! Like that girl over there.

Can you talk to her first?

Hello!
I'm Pips.

This is my friend Arlo. He's new in town.

Oh, hi, Arlo! Noice to meet you. I'm Marla.

Just like humans, crows from different groups have different accents and they adapt to "fit in"!

Would you like to join me for lunch at the baseball field?

With pleasure!

Humans waste 1.3 billion tons of food every year. I can't believe it, either.

Sorry, Pips. I know hot dogs aren't your thing.
Why's that?
I'm vegetarian.

That's okay, I found one piece of popcorn, so I'm full.

I'm thirsty, though.
Yeah, me too.

Marla, is there . . . ?

Yeah, there's a bottle of water over here.

Thanks!

Hmm.

My beak is too big.
It can't reach the
water.

Let me help you.

This rock will do.
?

PLOP!

Crows do that!

That's so

SMART!

Ha ha! Thanks.
Don't forget to drink.
Oh, right.
SLUURP!
Aah! That's
the best water
I ever drank!

?

Hey, Marla, what's that on your leg?

Crows are so smart that scientists love to observe and study them.

Crows are very curious; they always want to learn. That's how they get so smart.

THE
LAB

When I was a kid, I hurt my wing and I couldn't fly.
A woman named Ani rescued me and took care of me.
She was an ornithologist.
A WHAT?
A scientist.
Ornithologists are scientists who study birds.

She was nice, and she fed me lots of snacks.
Catch!

She played a lot of games with me.

Crows love to play! I've seen videos of crows snowboarding on slanted roofs, playing on a seesaw. . . . And bird species that like to play are very rare!

Some of those puzzles were so hard.

We also played tic-tac-toe.

And she taught me some circus tricks, just for fun.

Crows have solved very complex puzzles that even monkeys couldn't figure out!

She also taught me a bunch of human words.

Like what?

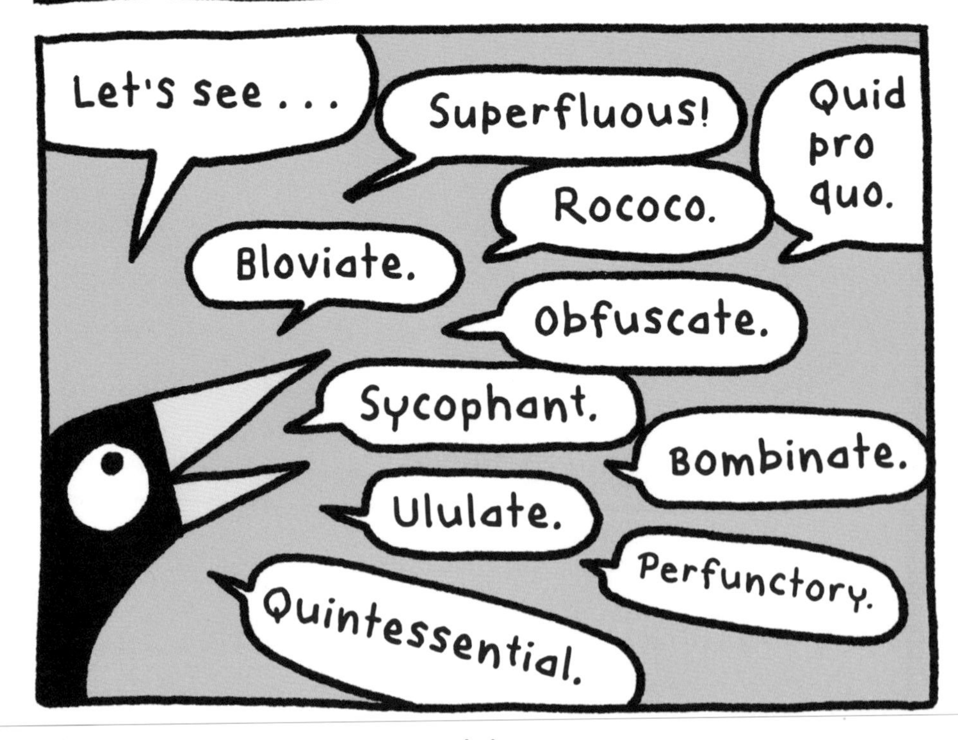
Let's see . . .
Superfluous!
Quid pro quo.
Rococo.
Bloviate.
Obfuscate.
Sycophant.
Bombinate.
Ululate.
Perfunctory.
Quintessential.

Crows remember humans who were nice to them. So . . . be nice to them!

In fact, I think I'll go say hi right now.

See you around . . . ?

Hope so!
Bye!

SIGH

FLOP!

What are you doing?

Marla is so SMART.

Smarter than ME, even.

I didn't even know it was POSSIBLE to be smarter than me!
Here we go again.
Pips . . .

I think I'm in
LOVE.

What do people do when they're in love?

I don't know, Arlo. You're the smart one.

Love is making my brain all sluggish. I can't think.

Maybe I should tell her how amazing I am?

How handsome, how clever, how muscular, how funny, how . . .
Arlo.

That's a BAD idea. Nobody likes show-offs.

But I'm the best show-off of all time!
That's for sure.

Oh, I know! I should perform my flying acrobatics!
She'll be SUPER impressed.

Watch this.

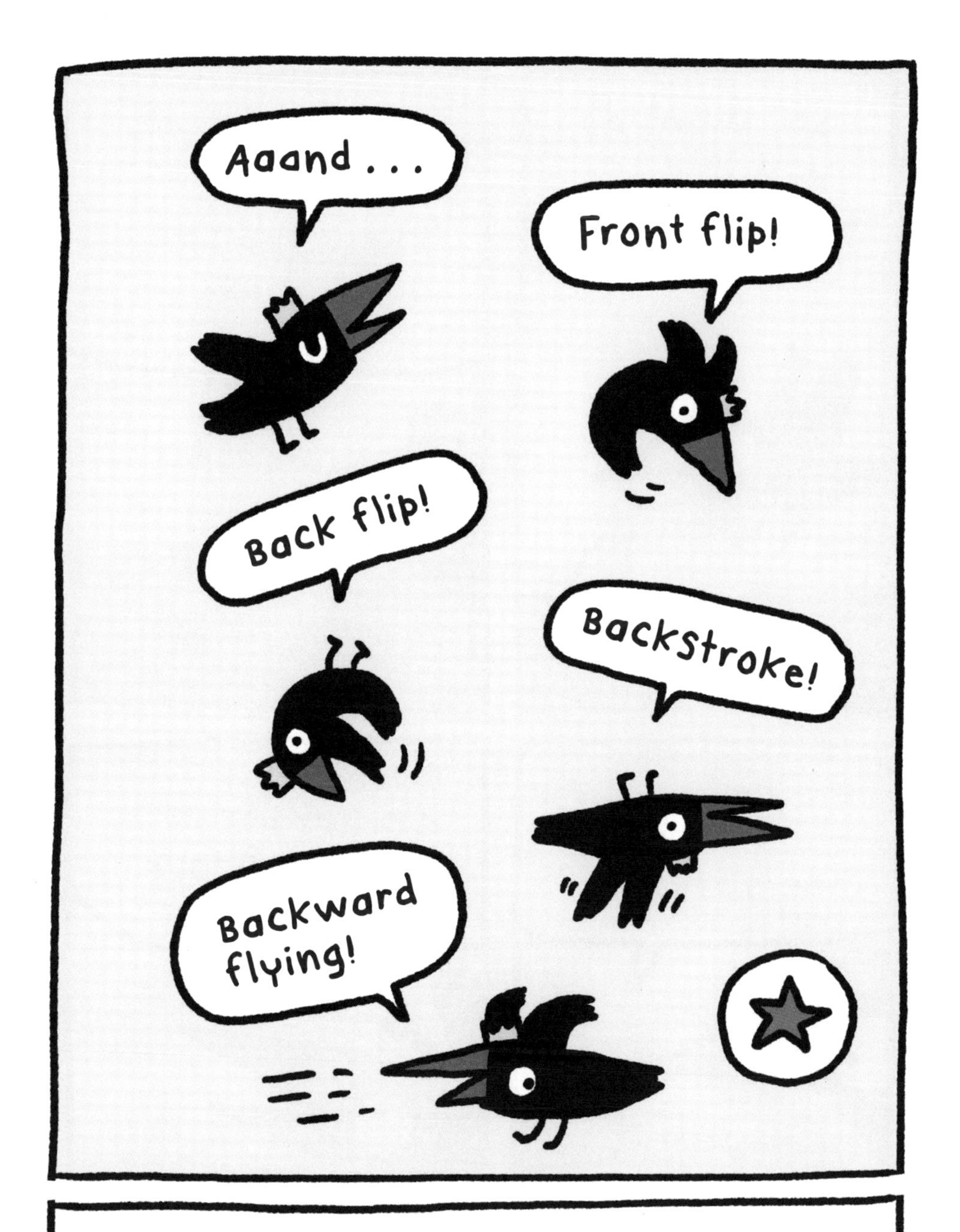

Crows are amazing acrobats, and enjoy doing tricks.

So? What do you think?

Impressive! But how do you know she likes acrobatics?

Maybe you should give her a present?

Oooh! That's a great idea! EVERYONE loves PRESENTS!

I'll go look through my collection!
I'll come with you.

Whoa. It got bigger since the last time I saw it!

Now, let's see . . . what should I give her?

A button? Boring. An earring? Not original. A painted toenail? Nah.

Oh! I know. I'll give her this!

What is it?

It's a die. Look. You throw it . . .

. . . and then you count the dots on top.

One, two, three, four, five.
That's a five!

You can applaud now.
Pff.

Aren't dice amazing?
Too complicated for me. . . .
I think she'll like it. I'll wrap it in a leaf . . .
. . . and I'll write her a card to go with it.
I didn't know crows could write.
They can't.

Here—what do you think?
Dear Marla,
You are smarter than a monkey and you know big words and I like you more than shiny things.
Arlo

Very romantic.

I know, right? I'm a genius poet.

Let's go see if she's back!

Oh, there she is!

Arlo's got something for you!
What is it?

Open it!

OMG, OMG, is it what I think it is?

 Crows can't read, either.

POK!
EWWW!
Stop that!
They lived happily ever after and had a bunch of babies.

THE END

No, but seriously, they will live happily ever after, which you will find out about in our third book.